Run
Away
Success

Peter Marney

ISBN-13: 978-1976373473
ISBN-10: 1976373476

This one's for the techies.

Read this first

You are not a ninja.

It's very important that you know this fact.

It's very important because, if you try to copy any of the stuff in this book, you might end up in hospital.

Even if you copy just some of this stuff you'll end up in trouble and maybe even in prison.

This will be bad.

This will be very bad because I'll get the blame.

So please, remember you're not a ninja and promise not to try and copy any of this stuff.

Have you promised?

Ok, you can now read on.

Keys

I blame Red.

She's my best friend but she can sometimes be forgetful about keys and stuff. That's why we're trying to break into her house.

Don't worry, we won't get caught.

We're good at this kind of thing and anyway, we've got Keira watching out for us.

They call me Jamie by the way and I'm a Red Sock Ninja. That's if our Ninja Clan keeps going.

After last night I was worried that we might not ever see each other again let alone keep our Clan together.

For reasons too complicated to explain right now we have to run away and hide from some very bad people. But, if we're to escape, Red needs more clothes as apparently a girl can't exist with just one pair of shoes. Did you know that?

How did we get in this mess?

It's a long story but basically it's sort of my fault.

Some time ago I tried to stop the Monster Twins from bullying Red which is a bit of a joke 'cos she's probably the best fighter in the school.

I didn't know that small fact at the time so trying to save her seemed the right thing to do and anyway, it all worked out ok 'cos me and Red got to become friends.

It's Red who first called me the Red Sock Ninja by the way. Yes, I know it's a silly name but I kind of like it.

Then Keira arrived.

I'm never sure how to describe Keira because she's complicated and, just when I think I've got her worked out, she does something new to surprise me.

It all started when she turned up one night as a babysitter, despite the fact that at ten years old I'm definitely not a baby, and it became a regular job for her twice a week after that.

Only now I've found out that Dad had sent her to keep an eye on us and that really she's a sort of spy like him which explains all of the odd things she knows and the strange skills she's taught us.

I mean, how many people do you know who can break into houses? Ok, maybe you shouldn't answer that question.

Talking of breaking in, could you hold on a moment? I've got to balance on this ledge while Red forces the lock on the window.

"Give me a hand Jamie, it's a bit stiff. It was the same last week when I broke in and I've been meaning to oil it."

Last week? How often does she forget her keys? Talk about a bad memory.

Sorry if I'm being a bit snappy this morning but we've not had a good couple of days.

Keira's keeping watch in case we get disturbed but it's the middle of the day and everyone should be out at school or work. Red wanted to say goodbye to her Mum and explain things properly but instead, with Keira's help, she's written a letter which will have to do for now.

We both wobble a bit as the catch snaps open and I grab something to stop myself falling. Then Red swings the window open and we slip inside.

She knows where everything is of course, and can grab what she needs without behaving like a proper burglar, but there's always something that goes missing or gets borrowed by one of her brothers or a visiting cousin. She says it happens all the time so she's sort of got used to it, just like her brothers have got used to being thumped when she finds out what they've nicked.

While Red's gathering her clothes and shoes, I sneak downstairs and put the letter on the kitchen table.

"Jamie?"

Now what's she forgot?

I run upstairs and find her holding a floorboard and looking into an empty hole.

"It's my secret place," she explains. "Where I hide stuff I don't want my brothers to see."

I've got to ask.

"So why's it empty then? No secrets at the moment?"

Red shakes her head. She's got lots of secrets and they're all in her diary. The diary that's not here.

"Where is it then?" I ask, looking around the room.

And that's why we're now at a different house and trying to break in through a different window.

At least this one's on the ground floor.

I really must have a word with Naz or her Mums. These locks are rubbish. The ones on the doors aren't much better either.

Here's a tip if you ever have to burgle somewhere.

Always unlock the doors.

That way, you've got a quick escape route if you need it. Nothing more embarrassing for a ninja than to get caught trying to break out of the home you've just broken into. Not that you should be breaking into strange houses of course. You're not a ninja, remember.

I don't like breaking into places and I especially don't like doing it in daylight. I know we've got a good reason and Naz won't mind but a nosey neighbour or the police might take a different view. We've had far too much to do with the police after yesterday and I'd be very happy if they don't turn up just now please.

Red's gone upstairs to find her diary and I'm sneaking a peek out of the front window just in case. We figure that, as the bad guys now have our photographs, it won't be long before they come after us. Naz wasn't there last night but, as Red's friend, she might get a visit just in case we happen to turn up.

That's when I see the van.

It's just pulled up and parked across the road. A big white minivan very like the one our new friends were going to use to kidnap us last night. Maybe I'm wrong and it's only a builder picking up his mate but he's just sitting there and waiting.

I jump as Keira silently creeps in through the back door giving a warning whistle.

"We've got company."

I nod and point out of the window.

"No, I meant out back. Two blokes in a car."

Time to lock the doors again I think.

We retreat upstairs to get a better look out of the windows and, as we appear to be surrounded, get ready for Plan B.

Plan B's the one where we have this really cool way of escaping with nobody following us. It does have a small problem though.

It doesn't exist.

I think we're trapped.

Peter Marney

Trapped

If this was an action film, there'd be a secret passage or tunnel out of the house which would take us to a waiting speedboat or fast car.

Then there'd be this exciting chase with lots of shooting and crashes and near misses but without anyone actually getting hurt. You know the sort of thing.

But this isn't a film and I get the horrible feeling that we're definitely going to get hurt just as soon as our friends outside decide to come inside and get us. Keira says that they're probably waiting for reinforcements; more men to help capture and kidnap us.

Oh goody!

Another car's just pulled up outside and more people are getting out.

This is probably more bad news but it turns out I'm wrong. The cavalry have arrived to rescue us!

Well, Naz and her Mums have come home which is a sort of a rescue as I expect the bad guys won't want to make a move now we've got company.

Keira and me stay upstairs on guard while Red waits for our rescuers to get in and shut the door before making her entrance.

"Hi Naz, hello Paula, Joan. Sorry to break in but I needed my diary a bit urgent like. Oh, by the way, don't stare out of the window but I think someone may be after us."

They take it well.

"Us?" asks Paula.

"Yeah, Keira and Jamie's upstairs watching them."

They know Keira and I've visited a couple of times.

"I'll put the kettle on," says Joan, "then I think you'd better tell us the whole story."

So she did and we did.

Well, Keira told most of it and sort of didn't quite say that she maybe, might, sort of be employed by our Secret Service so it's all sort of all right.

Paula puts down her mug.

"So, you found the bombers and fed the information back but nothing's been done about it except that suddenly you're being chased by both sides. Something's not right here."

Yeah, we'd kind of figured that out for ourselves.

"Keira, I think you're right. You all need to escape and disappear for a while. I assume that any safe houses you know are also known to your bosses?"

Keira nods.

How does Paula know about safe houses?

I know I'm only a kid and people don't bother telling me everything but is everyone a spy?

Dad being a spy is sort of ok and not too much of a surprise if I think about it, which I never did by the way. I mean, parents are supposed to be boring and embarrassing and not have really cool and exciting jobs. Having a spy for a Dad isn't how it's supposed to work is it?

And then my freaky babysitter also turns out to be a spy as well. It's too much!

Actually and when I think about it, nobody's said that out aloud. Keira's not admitted she's a spy and Dad never actually said so either. But he did send her to protect us and you don't learn all of her strange skills working in a shop or an office do you?

I'm also fairly sure that the Army don't let skinny blonde girls into the SAS so I think I'm sticking with "spy" unless you can think of a better explanation.

"So, you need a proper escape plan and somewhere to run. Any ideas?" asks Paula.

Keira knows a man with a boat who can get us away but we've not got passports so that might turn tricky. Better to stay in the country and hide until Dad can sort things out with his boss.

Joan's looking thoughtful.

"I've got a friend up North who runs a school. Might be a good place to hide. She takes a few boarders so they'd not be suspicious if you've got a good story."

Paula looks doubtful.

"You really think Jamie would fit in?"

What? It's an all girls school or something?

They both look me up and down. Whatever they're looking for, it seems I haven't got it.

Paula frowns.

"If they're really outside in that van, then they know about Naz as well. We can look after ourselves and my office can pull a few strings but I'd be happier if Naz was somewhere safer for a while."

I grin at Naz and she grins back. Looks like she's joining us on our new adventure. I like adventures even if it means going to yet another new school.

As there's a chance that our friends outside may have bugged the phones, we agree that Joan'll call her friend from somewhere else to set up our visit. We get sent upstairs to keep watch while the grown ups work out the details.

Why do adults think they have to organise everything?

Naz has got out her telescope and we can see right inside the front of the van. Looks like the guy's got a camera with a long lens on it to take snaps of us if we show ourselves.

I think I've got an idea.

Joan picks up the phone.

"Hello? Police? I'm sorry if this sounds silly but I think there's some odd chap outside trying to take photos of my daughter and her friends. He's just sitting there in his van playing with his camera. What? Ok, thanks."

A few minutes later and our waiting friend is talking to a couple of interested policemen. Joan goes out to join them while the rest of us get into Paula's car and drive off, making sure to avoid going anywhere near the alley entrance where the other car's still waiting.

Phase One complete.

Now we need to meet up with Joan at the agreed spot so she can phone her friend.

On the way Keira briefs us on our cover story. If we're going into hiding we've got to pretend to be someone else.

It's a good cover story and I don't like it one little bit.

A new start

Things are going right for a change and Joan's friend agrees to hide us at her school.

I could tell you where we're going but then I'd have to kill you. Sorry about that but it's the sort of thing us spies do all the time.

Seriously though, I've no idea where we are. They did mention the name of the place we're going to but it didn't mean anything to me. I've never been much good at geography or maps.

I could also tell you how we got here but that's a secret too. We might have to use the same trick again later and I don't want the wrong people reading this and learning our tradecraft. That's another spy word and means how we do stuff.

How do I know all of this?

It's a long drive and Keira's chatting to keep herself awake. I'm learning all sorts of things.

We arrive after dark and Joan's friend, Miss Rainey, meets us at the flat we've been given. Hope it's got a loo, I'm busting!

I miss part of Miss Rainey's welcome speech but catch up, much relieved, a few minutes later. The girls and Keira seem happy enough so I guess everything's ok. All I want to do now is grab something to eat and get to bed.

There's a box of food on the kitchen table so, after Miss Rainey leaves, we help Keira make a snack and a drink.

Over a sandwich, Keira reminds us of our cover story and I still don't like it.

It's been a long day and all I want to do is sleep. At least I get a room to myself, even if I can touch both walls when I stretch.

Why's Keira shaking me?

"Come on sleepyhead, time for school!"

How can it be time for school, I've only just nodded off and besides, where's Dad?

It takes me a few moments to properly wake up and remember where I am and what's going on. Then everything's a rush as we need to get washed, fed and round to the school before eight.

What?

Did someone just say eight?

What time is that to start school? I'm usually still asleep at eight. What sort of school starts at eight?

Must be a mufti day or something as Keira gets us dressed in our gym kit and then we're all straight off to school.

It's only a short walk and I try to remember the route. Must say the town doesn't look any better by daylight and the school looks a bit of a dump as well which I guess is a good thing as nobody's going to be looking for us here.

We're taken straight to see Miss Rainey and her office is just as untidy as the one at our old school. Guess all head teachers have to have messy desks as part of the job except that I've got it wrong and Miss Rainey is a Principal and not a Head.

"So sorry I can't give you a guided tour but it's all been a bit of a rush since your mother phoned, Naz. Probably best if we get you all into class and sort something out later."

I'd much rather have a look around by myself anyway. See what sort of locks they have on the doors and windows and that sort of thing. Ok, I know that's not normal but I'm a secret ninja, remember?

Keira gets to go back to the flat or whatever and we get taken to our first lesson which is in the gym.

Brilliant!

I might not have mentioned it, but I've learned to love gyms since Keira got me into boxing. She said I needed to be able to defend myself which is very true in case I ever accidentally upset Red.

Guess it's her growing up with three big brothers and lots of cousins that makes Red such a good fighter. I suppose you have to get good if you want to keep your stuff from being nicked and she's very good.

That's odd.

There's a piano in the gym.

Why would you keep a piano in a gym? What's wrong with a beatbox if you need some music? And why are there mirrors on the walls?

Maybe they're into karate and need to check out their kicks and stuff. This is going to be so cool. I love karate and have wanted to learn it properly for ages.

Something's definitely not right here.

Some old lady has just sat down at the piano and another one, not quite so old, has brought the rest of the class in from the changing room. There's a complete lack of boxing gloves or trainers and rather more leotards and those little slipper things girls wear.

I reckon this is some sort of dippy keep fit class.

"To your positions girls and boys!" shouts the teacher holding this stick thing. Yes, there's a couple of boys wearing those silly slippers as well.

Naz and the rest of the class move to the walls leaving me and Red stood the middle.

"Ah yes, Miss Rainey did mention that we had some new pupils joining us this morning. I'm Miss Langley-Brown and you will call me Madame."

She's giving us the same up and down look which Naz's Mums gave me and she's equally unimpressed.

"I suppose it's too much to hope that you've any advanced grades?"

We look blank.

"They haven't Madame," says Naz from beside the mirror.

She's always been quicker on the uptake than me. I'd have called her

25

Miss like I always call teachers, even the men ones sometimes.

"I've grade three classical and grade two modern," says Naz.

Madame sort of sighs.

"Oh, modern."

What's wrong with modern? Sounds better than old.

Madame then gives me another look, just to make sure.

"Well, go and stand over there. You can't join in wearing those things!"

What's wrong with my trainers?

"Thank you Mrs Frobisher."

That's when the music starts and I realise just how deep a mess I'm in.

I'm a prisoner in a ballet class!

Gorillas and giraffes

I've decided I hate Naz.

She knows this stuff and is joining in with the other girls, hanging off of this bar thing while me and Red stand here like lemons.

What do I know about ballet?

About as much as I know about gorillas. I know they exist and I'm very happy they exist somewhere else and have nothing to do with me. Mind you, I feel a bit like a gorilla at the moment looking at some of the graceful moves going on around me.

Bet none of them would last five minutes in a boxing ring though, apart from Naz. She's good enough to go a few rounds with Red without getting damaged.

As we're doing nothing useful, me and Red slide across to the notice board and try to pick up some information about our new school. I leave the reading stuff to Red and just stand and watch everyone.

I've never seen proper ballet before but I've seen a lot of boxers so I can sort of judge people. A couple definitely know what they're doing but there's a few strugglers and one or two looking a bit giraffe like. Tall, thin and gawky. Maybe they've got long black tongues as well. I'll have to check later.

The teacher's got her eye on us and wanders over while she keeps telling the dancers what to do next.

"I suppose it's too much to ask if you've any dance training at all is it?"

I shake my head.

"No Miss, I mean Madame."

Red does a bit of breakdancing but I don't suppose she wants to know about that.

She does her sigh thing again and turns back to the class. I get the feeling that we're not going to be friends.

What a great start to the day.

At least she leaves us alone for the rest of the lesson which seems pretty short for a training session. I wonder if it's got anything to do with her limp?

She's hiding it well but I think she's injured. She spent the first part of the lesson prodding girls with her stick thing but then retreated to the piano for support.

Not that I'm supposed to, but I notice these little things.

It's like in boxing. You keep watching your opponent for any weaknesses you can attack. She's putting more weight on her right leg which means the left one is injured.

In the ring I'd start running about to get her moving to her left as much as possible and weaken it further but here she's in charge and so just calls a finish to the lesson. Everyone gets sent off to shower, as if they need it, and they all leave.

You'd expect a few questions, being new like, but all the girls seem more interested in Naz than us when they come out of the changing rooms so we just tag along.

Seems Naz has suddenly got a new father.

"No, Daddy really wanted me back in the UK. The local schools were just too awful and there's so little to do."

Guess she's improvising on our cover story.

Naz and Red are supposed to be newly arrived back in the UK. Keira says to keep it vague if we can and sort of hint at the need for secrecy for diplomatic reasons. No, I've no idea what that means either.

I'm supposed to have been sent here by an aunt and I've only just met the girls as we're having to share a flat with our new housemother (that's Keira apparently). In case you're wondering, we've all got new haircuts as well as part of our disguise. Red says my crop makes me look like a real fighter, a proper thug. Is that a good thing do you think?

This is the bit I don't like. Naz is supposed to be rich and Red is her sort of playmate servant or something. She hands Red her bag without even looking and just walks off chatting with her new blonde friends.

Normally Red would throw it straight back at her but normally Naz wouldn't do it anyway. It's all part of our cover.

"Kate?"

Oh, we've got new names as well.

"Yes Natalia?"

Why does Naz get the posh name?

"Find out where our lockers are dear and lose that, would you?"

I can see Red clench her fists and lips at the same time. Someone's going to pay for this later when we can find a proper gym.

Some boy gives me a nudge.

"I'll show you where to go," he says.

"Thanks," I mumble automatically.

He looks a bit like me but taller and with longer hair. Let's face it, everyone's got longer hair than me at the moment!

"My name's Harrison but everyone calls me Harry. You're?"

He leaves a space in the conversation.

"Jay," I say.

It's supposed to be short for Jayden but I don't think he wants to know that.

Keira says it's best to have a name sort of like your own in case any of us slip up and use our real names.

He nods and I'm happy to let him chat.

"Don't worry about them."

He sort of waves at the backs of the departing girls.

"They're all right but a bit stuck up. Everyone's gossiping about the new girls and making up stories. Is she really a princess?"

I shake my head.

"Don't think so."

As if I know anything about princesses.

"Thought not. Too obvious. I bet she's some sort of spy or secret ninja."

I'm trying to keep a blank face. How does he know?

"Ok, that's supposed to be a joke."

I breath again.

"Thought so," I lie. "I mean, look at them. They're girls, and Princess there has just spent the last ten minutes prancing around like a demented pixie. Hardly spy-like is it?"

He looks a bit deflated.

Oops!

I've just remembered that he's also been prancing about like a pixie. Maybe this isn't the best way to make friends. Let's try again.

"I don't think she really knows what she's doing. Not like you. Madame whatsit didn't have to poke her stick at you so I guess you're a bit good at this stuff."

He just nods.

We arrive at some lockers and Red chucks Naz's, I mean Nat's, stuff in an empty one at the end.

"I can teach you the basics if you like. Lend you some shoes."

Like I want to learn ballet?

But Keira said we need to fit in so I force a grin onto my face.

"Yes please!"

Looks like I'm going to be a ballerina.

Peter Marney

New friends

The rest of the morning is filled with the usual boring school stuff but we have to work a bit longer and only have a five minute break for a snack and no playtime.

I manage to bump into Red a couple of times and get chatting like we don't really know each other yet but might become friends.

All of this pretending is hard work!

Lunch is in this cafe type place at the back of the building but the food's ok and it gives me another chance to bump into Red.

Natalia is sitting with her new friends and I get the feeling that we're not going to be invited to join them. Instead, Harry calls us over to another table and, as we sit, he introduces us to everyone.

"This is Em and Tippy," he says, "and he's Jonny, Tip's little brother."

What sort of name is Tippy for a girl? Must be a nickname. Maybe she falls over a lot. She certainly looked a bit wobbly in that ballet class and Em wasn't much better. A bit giraffe like. Do you think she'll poke out her tongue if I ask her?

"Do we call you Katherine or is it Katrina?" Em asks Red.

They know our names already? How do they know our names? I can't even remember our names.

Jonny's got a better idea.

"Cat," he says. "We should call her Cat. She moves like a cat."

Someone else who's good at noticing things. We'll have to be careful with him.

Most people see what they want to see, which is good if you're a secret ninja because we don't want people to notice us. Keira's trained us to disappear in a crowd; to stay unnoticed.

We're also good at pretending not to be looking when we're really interested in something. That's why I'm not looking at Jonny. I think I'm going to not be looking at Jonny for a while.

For some reason the name Cat has started them all laughing and so, joining in, Red agrees to be called Cat. Then she starts gossiping to find out about our new home. Teachers, subjects, who's good and who's bitchy. All useful stuff.

She's good at this chatting thing and much better than me.

It's Red who finds out that the chief blondie is called Tammy. Tamara Crowley-Wolff, or Growley-Dog behind her back. Her sidekicks are Abby and Jo and now I guess Nat who seems to have fitted right in with the blondies despite her black hair.

Ah, now I see what they were laughing at.

Growley-Dog and Red Cat!

I suppose it's a sort of joke but it's too late to join in the laughter. I'm not very good with jokes by the way so, if you notice any more, can you give me a nudge please so I know when to laugh. Red usually does that for me but she's on the other side of the table and busy gossiping.

By the whispers and looks from the top table I guess that Naz is also getting the lowdown on the school and from the sneers and giggles I reckon that the blondies aren't being too nice about my new friends.

Before Red can find out any more juicy information, the bell goes and everyone starts to leave. The blondies just pick up their bags and leave their mess on the table. On their way past, Dog Girl gives a loud sniff and a puzzled look before walking off with her mates. Why do I think she's up to something?

Looking about, I see a waste bin and take my rubbish over and tip it away. I don't care what the rest do but nobody's being my servant. Red does the same and then we're off into the Hall to meet another new teacher.

Mr Duval is small and like a wasp. All buzzy, annoying, and with a sting in his tail. He's supposed to be teaching us acting but it's more all about how useless we are.

He gets us each to walk across the room like someone different.

"Maybe a dancer, an invalid, a shop assistant, a princess."

For some reason he glances at Naz while he gives that last suggestion but she ignores him just like a proper princess would when faced with some minor servant.

What's with this princess thing anyway? Where did that rumour come from and why's it causing all this fuss?

I mean, Naz and Red are more or less the same, apart from the hair. Both girls, both new. But it's Naz who's getting all of the attention just because somebody thinks she might be a princess. How does that make her different?

We start doing our pretend walks one at a time and some are quite funny although nobody laughs. It's all done in complete silence except for Mr Duval's waspy comments.

"Is that dancer or invalid dear? I can't tell the difference."

"Does anyone really walk like that?"

"Do you know, I'm almost certain I didn't ask for gorilla?"

That one's aimed at Red and I can see she's getting angry. It's not good to get Red angry and, if he's not careful, Mr Waspy's about to find out why.

She marches right up to him and glares into his eyes which is easy to do as he's not that much taller than her.

"No sir, you didn't ask for gorilla and I wasn't doing gorilla."

She's standing too close to him and they both know it. I can see he's trying to look taller. He's also sort of leaning back but pretending not to move.

It's just like before a fight. A stand off.

You stand there, measuring up the other guy and trying to outstare them. Do it right and you can win the fight even before you land the first punch.

This is not going to end well.

Princess

Maybe punching Mr Waspy isn't a good idea even if he does deserve it what with his nasty comments and everything.

Time for me to do something good before Red does something bad and gets us expelled from the school before we've even properly started.

"Do you want me to try sir?" I ask, cartwheeling into a space before he has the chance to answer.

"I can't do gorilla sir but this is my starfish."

I cartwheel a bit more and the rest of the class laugh. Red turns away from Mr Waspy who's now shouting at me.

"Do you think that's funny, boy?"

Well, yes I hope so. That's the idea but I suppose I'd better not admit it.

"No sir," I say innocently.

Naz joins in to rescue me.

"Please Sir, can you show us what you mean? Sometimes it's better for some of us to see it done properly. We rarely see an expert actor performing."

That gets a sort of smile from him and Mr Waspy starts to show off. Actually he's not bad as an actor. Just rubbish as a teacher.

Maybe there's some use to Naz being the posh princess after all.

I notice that Mr Waspy starts glancing at her like a dog doing tricks and looking for praise from his owner. Maybe that's why he doesn't like me. I'm rubbish with dogs.

He must be a good actor because he's now acting like Red didn't nearly punch him and has gone back to his waspy comments but none aimed in our direction. In fact he starts to act as if me and Red aren't even in the room any more which is fine by me.

Don't want to be an actor anyway.

Mind you, I suppose some of these skills could be useful to a secret ninja. I mean, we already sort of act when we're secretly following someone. You know, pretending to just be going in the same direction and suddenly deciding to look in this shop window if our target stops to have a look around.

The sound of the bell snaps me out of my daydream and we're off again to the next class which is singing and for once I'm not rubbish.

Apparently I've got a good voice but it needs training. Hope that's not like Keira's boxing training which had me running around the streets at night chasing after her.

That seems so long ago.

I wonder how everyone is at home. Not that I've got a home what with Mum away resting and Dad on the run. Not quite how I expected things to turn out but nothing in my life seems to turn out normal these days.

I blame Keira but not too much. If I upset her, my new housemother might stop feeding me!

It's been a strange day but I think I've ended up about even.

I've got two teachers who definitely don't like me but one singing teacher who does. I guess Miss Rainey might like me as well so that sort of makes it a draw.

Naz's new snooty set of blondies don't really count as far as I'm concerned but I may have a friend in Harry and the others aren't so bad.

All in all, it's sort of ok for a first day if you ignore Red nearly having a fight with Mr Waspy.

Keira collects us from school, full of questions, but Naz just walks ahead still being the princess.

Me and Red give Keira a cut down version of the news and an assessment of the security.

You think we were doing nothing during those lessons?

A good ninja always looks at what's around them.

"No alarm systems but not much worth nicking anyway," I say.

Red agrees.

"Windows are a bit Toy Town but the doors have some good locks on them. I reckon we'd have no trouble getting in or out though."

We like breaking into school. Gives us somewhere to train as ninjas.

We chat a bit more about our day and then we're back to the flat and Naz still hasn't said a word.

We're through the front door and she suddenly bursts into tears and throws her arms around Red.

"Red, it's horrible! I was horrible! I hate it!"

Keira sensibly puts the kettle on while Red just stands there hugging Naz until she's cried out.

Sometimes being a friend just means being there without having to say anything.

Well, that's what Red says. I've never really got the friend thing myself although Red's teaching me, even if I'm a bit thick when it comes to all this people stuff.

While we were busy getting annoyed at Naz and getting into trouble with teachers, I hadn't even thought about how she was getting on. I mean, she seemed to have made new friends quickly enough.

Then the phone rings and Keira answers it.

Sounds like we've already had a complaint and I'm guessing it's from Mr Waspy.

Keira agrees with Miss Rainy that it's all probably down to the shock of moving into a new school and everything and she promises to have a word with us.

Seems like none of us have had a good first day after all.

Over a cup of tea, we calm Naz down and I lie and tell her that I wasn't upset and knew she was just pretending. This is going to be a bit more difficult than we thought.

Naz wants to quit but that's never the answer.

"We quit when we've got somewhere better to go or if we get found out," says Keira.

It makes sense. No point in running off like headless chickens just 'cos it's a challenge.

"As I see it Naz," says Red, "we've got two choices. Either you keep up the act or you change it. Stay with the blondies or come join the misfits."

Naz doesn't agree.

"Mum Paula says it's never about two choices. People always want to make things simple. Always saying either or. Either do this or you'll have to do that. Life's never that simple. There's always more choices."

Guess we just need to figure out what these other choices are then.

Feet

We're back at school and under strict instructions from Keira to fit in or else she'll kill us.

I think she's joking.

Well, I hope she's joking.

Harry has agreed with Madame that he'll try and teach me the basics of this ballet stuff and I've asked him to teach Red as well. That's why we're here in the corner in borrowed slippers and I'm learning to stand like a duck.

Did you know that feet have positions?

Mine just go side by side but that's all wrong apparently. Then there's arm positions and the head and the chest and everything else from top to toe. I can even manage to get things wrong just standing still.

Slowly and over the first couple of weeks, I begin to get the hang of the very basics and can at least stand like a dancer. Harry must be doing something right because Madame even gives me the occasional glance without doing one of her sighs.

Back in the changing room, Dog Girl starts sniffing again.

"There's an odd smell in here," she says. "I have a very sensitive nose you know."

It will be when I punch it.

Sorry, but I'm getting fed up with the blondies and the way they think they own the school. I'm beginning to think that they're not very nice people.

She keeps giving the odd sniff now and again throughout the week and, although she never says anything, I get the distinct feeling that she's getting at me.

"Do I smell?" I ask Red.

She takes a sniff.

"Yes Jamie."

Oh!

"But no more than anyone else. It's a nice sort of Jamie smell."

Whew, that's ok then.

The next day the other blondies start getting in on the act with the occasional comment in class.

"Please Miss, can we have a window opened?"

"Please Sir, can I move desks?"

I think I should hit someone but Red decides we need to talk to Kiera first.

She gives me a sniff as well.

"Smells ok to me. I think they're just being horrible," she says.

Well, duh!

Then she smiles.

I think she has a plan.

Well, I hope she has a plan, otherwise we're breaking into school for no reason.

Yes, we're back in our dark clothes and sneaking through bushes around the back of the building before attacking one of those Toy Town window locks.

If you think they're rubbish, you should see what's guarding our lockers. Even a baby could open one of those locks with her nappy pin.

While Red's fiddling with Dog Girl's locker, Kiera is very

carefully opening up a small bottle she's taken from a pocket.

"We used to use this trick when I was at school," she says.

Keira went to school?

"Red, lift out those ballet shoes would you please?"

She then gently plops three drops into each shoe.

"No smell, no colour, but don't touch it or you'll soon wish you hadn't," she warns.

We put everything away, just as it was, and then it's back out the way we came in and off home.

It's so unfair!

We've gone through all of that risk and Keira won't even tell us what's going to happen to Dog Girl.

"Just go to school and act normally. You'll find out."

So that's what we do.

It's really hard not to watch someone when you know something's going to happen. I do sort of notice that she's just put on her ballet shoes without exploding or anything.

In fact, nothing happens at all except that she sniffs at me again on the way past into the dance studio. She's definitely being nasty.

Madame's halfway through her lesson when one of the blondies starts coughing.

"Please Miss, Jay smells and it's awful!"

She's right about the smell but it's not coming from me.

We all start sniffing and Miss has to stop everything and get us to stand still.

Then she walks around the room, backwards and forwards until she's standing in front of Dog Girl. She doesn't say anything but I reckon she's worked out where the smell's coming from.

She lets us open all of the windows but the smell just won't go away and so the lesson ends even earlier than usual and Madame tells all of us to take a shower.

Back in the changing room, the blondies all crowd together down one end as usual until Dog Girl takes off her shoes and then it's like a sudden people explosion. All of the girls quickly grab their towels and run of to their shower holding their breath.

Then the smell hits us and we do the same thing but with a bit more noise.

"Phew!"

"Yuk!"

"Has somebody stepped in something?"

When we come back, Dog Girl's still trying to blame me but her shoes are saying otherwise.

"Maybe you need fresh tights," Red says helpfully.

"Maybe she needs to wash her feet a bit more often," adds Tippy.

I don't think Tip likes Dog Girl or the teasing she gets from her.

Miss Growley-Wolff spends a long time in the shower and comes back to find that Madame has wrapped the ballet shoes in a plastic bag.

Nobody says anything and we all leave as quickly as we can but I do manage a loud sniff before I go. See how she likes it!

I think I've worked it out.

Doesn't show or smell but you mustn't touch it or else.

Well, we know what "or else" means and I reckon that the liquid must be heat sensitive. Whatever Keira dropped into the shoes starts to work when it gets hot. I wonder if it stops working when it gets cold again.

I decide it must do 'cos Dog Girl is back wearing the same shoes the next morning and they don't smell at all. Well, not until half way through the lesson again.

I didn't say anything, honest.

I just sort of sniffed as I looked at Dog Girl and she ran out of the room crying.

Madame gets Harry to take over the exercises and scurries after her. By the time we finish, Dog Girl is showered and the shoes are on the floor. I offer to spray them with the new deodorant Keira's got me but that doesn't help. Dog Girl just bursts out crying again.

Some girls are just too sensitive.

Peter Marney

Changes

Things are changing.

Little things.

Suddenly, Dog Girl isn't quite as popular as she used to be. People are beginning to keep their distance and even the blondies don't seem so keen for her company, especially after our dance class each morning.

Without even trying, Naz seems to have become the new Queen of the School and Dog Girl is reduced to just one of the crowd. Funny how the princess rumour and a few drops of a clear liquid can change things.

Of course, Miss Growley-Wolff doesn't like this new development and now snaps at everyone, teachers included, which makes her even less popular.

The only one still being nice to her is Naz who has decided to be nice to everyone and forget the mask of our cover story. It makes her happier and also stops Red from wanting to punch someone now she's not being treated as a servant.

All should be right with our world but it isn't.

We're in trouble.

Dog Girl is really getting upset, crying and all sorts of stuff, and Naz is blaming me and Keira.

"Yes, I know she was being horrid to you Jamie but this has gone too far. She's talking about giving up dancing and maybe even leaving the school."

I don't see the problem. I think school'll be better off without her and I know a few people who'd agree with me. Keira doesn't seem too bothered either.

"Actions have consequences Naz. You do something nasty and there's going to be some payback eventually. Well, she just got hers."

I know Naz is supposed to be Queen Blondie now but I think she's going too far and needs to stick up for her real friends.

"If you don't like it, just tell her to throw the shoes away," suggests Red.

That's a good idea.

"And how do I explain why I know that it's the shoes causing the smell?" asks Naz.

Ok, maybe it's not such a good idea.

"She got those shoes as a present from her father before her parents got divorced and he moved out. It's all she's got left of him now that he's gone abroad," says Naz.

I didn't know that.

"Then she'll just have to wait for the smell to wear off," says Keira in a tone of voice which suggests this conversation is finished.

Maybe we did go a bit far but I still think she deserved it, don't you?

Anyway, I'm fed up with all this pretending. I'm still having trouble remembering that Red is supposed to be Kate and have called her by the wrong name twice this week. Lucky for us, we were alone both times.

Naz's name isn't so bad but I don't get to talk to her much at school anyway what with her popularity and everything.

With her suddenly becoming a pretend Mum to us three, you'd think Keira would also be getting fed up but she doesn't say anything. Actually she seems quite happy in a Keira sort of way which is odd.

I worry when Keira gets happy as it usually means we're about to get into trouble.

With not much to do in the flat, Keira tells us that she's been wandering the town and finding out where everything is and how it all connects. Any good ninja's got to know their surroundings and how to get about the place without attracting attention.

She's even found us a gym of sorts.

We're too young to join but she's managed to get us a couple of practise sessions a week before the real fighters finish work and get started. It's got all the right kit and I can thrash away at a punching bag as much as I want.

Keira even lets me fight her and lands me on the ground a couple of times to remind me that I'm still learning.

Naz gets to fight her as well which is how I notice what's going on. Keira's changing her fighting style to match each one of us and to test out our weak points.

Then the door opens and this tough guy walks in.

Like I said, I'm good at judging people and this one's a fighter. The tattoos are a bit of a clue as well.

He just stands there watching Keira and Naz.

"Heard we had a new fighter," he says. "Must have got it wrong."

Oops.

Keira stops and turns to him.

"Just training my girl," she says, "but I can give you a couple of rounds if you like."

He gives her one of those up and down looks and then laughs. He definitely doesn't know how to make friends.

"Not worth getting my gloves on is it," he sneers.

Keira grins.

"Fine by me."

Naz moves off the mat and Keira squares up to her new playmate. Hope he knows what he's doing. Actually, by the look of him he does, so I hope she knows what she's doing as well.

They circle each other carefully, looking for weaknesses and a chance to attack. He tries a punch which Keira easily ducks under, swerving to avoid the follow up jab to where her ribs should have been.

Somehow she turns the swerve into a drop and aims a kick to his head which he just manages to dodge. Then it's back to circling again and watching.

Suddenly they both attack and the mat is a whirl of flying arms and legs with both bodies moving all over the place.

I know Keira's good at this stuff but there's all sorts of styles coming out and the guy's matching her blow for blow and, because he's bigger and stronger, I think Keira's weakening and he's going to beat her.

Keira's going to get hurt.

Hold on a minute.

Nothing's landing!

By now I'd expect maybe some blood on the floor but they're both still unharmed.

They back away from each other, both watching and waiting for the next move. Then Keira suddenly rushes forward, throws herself at him and gives him a big hug.

What's going on?

She's never done that before.

Has Keira suddenly fallen in love?

Peter Marney

Trouble

Keira disengages herself from the tough guy and they're both grinning as she turns around.

"Say hello to Jack, my big bro."

Keira's got a brother?

So that's why she's such a good fighter; she's got a big brother.

We all say hello and then Jack takes us somewhere that does great chocolate milkshakes. I like him already.

I also notice he's good at not asking questions.

I don't know what Keira's told him but he just acts like it's normal for his sister to have three kids in tow and suddenly be here. I guess he doesn't know everything 'cos Keira's using our cover names.

"Yeah, Natalia and Kate are new here and I'm looking after them. Jay's just arrived as well and been put in our flat."

This gets a look from Jack but he doesn't say anything.

"Need any help?" he asks.

Do we look that much trouble?

"You know, best shops, places to avoid, people not to fight without being introduced first?"

He's laughing now.

"Seriously, if you need anything, just ask. I've got some lads who can help out if needed."

Oh, that sort of help. Maybe he does know the sort of stuff his little sister gets involved in.

Keira tells him to keep his ears open for any strange questions and then starts asking him about his life.

We let them get on with it and chat between ourselves about school.

We agree that Mr Waspy is useless and needs sorting out if he keeps trying to bully the class. Naz has also picked up on Madame's injury. Most dance classes are apparently at least three times as long and twice as hard so she knew something was wrong.

"Harry's the only real dancer there but he does solo sessions and works on his own after school."

I didn't know that. How does she know that? It's not even as though she's his friend or anything.

"The girls chat about him. I think they're a bit angry that he doesn't fancy any of them. I don't think they've come across many real ballet boys."

They're not the only ones but I kind of like him and he seems to like me and Red.

Keira's finished her family reunion so we slurp up the last of our milkshakes and head off home.

But it's not home is it.

I'm not supposed to notice but some mornings the girls look as if they've been crying and I know that Red's missing her Mum. That must go double for Naz as she's got two Mums.

My Dad's been on the phone a couple of times and keeps promising that it'll all soon be over but we're still here and here isn't there.

The good news is that nobody seems to be looking for us yet and we've got a new teacher.

"Good morning class. I'm afraid Madame won't be with us for a little while so I've been asked to step in. My name's Miss Gibbs."

It's a good job Madame's not here 'cos Miss Gibbs would already be in trouble. She's not standing like a duck.

"My ballet's a bit rusty so we'll move on to something more modern I think."

She pulls out this beat box from behind the piano and sets it going.

Now we're getting somewhere.

Miss Gibbs then spends twenty minutes on a proper warm up and I'm beginning to like it here. Some of the blondies are fading but us ninjas are just getting started. Harry's keeping up as well.

Then we have to form a circle and listen to the beat.

"Think how your body can move to this. Dance in your head."

I can see fear in some eyes. They're not used to thinking this early in the morning.

Then we each have to move into the middle and do a solo.

The first two girls just freeze but the next one at least tries to fit her ballet steps to the beat even if she fails badly. Then it's Red's turn and she's ready for it.

Before we got into boxing, Red did a bit of street dancing. She picks up the beat and spins into the middle with a handstand which turns into a couple of floor moves before she rolls up into a robot step back to place.

Miss G gives a cheer.

"That's more like it! Anyone else?"

Harry runs into the middle and leaps with his legs in split position before twisting to a landing and stepping around the circle and back to place. Naz follows him with a ninja roll and some kick boxing moves to the beat.

Miss G then gets us all moving.

"Think of a finish! Track's ending in 3,2,1 and stop!"

We're all out of breath and for the first time since getting here I feel like we've actually done some work. Everyone's sweating and two of the stick girls look like they're going to throw up.

Shame Dog Girl's not here; she would have hated it.

"Three minutes rest but keep moving. You don't want to stiffen up."

While the blondies get their breath back, Miss G tells us that we can expect the same for the next few weeks. She wants to teach us the dance routine from some musical she's been in so we've got words and tunes to learn once we've got the dance moves down.

"Fitness! It's no good just being able to dance for ten minutes. If you want to be any sort of dancer then you've got to be fit. You need to build up your dance muscles."

She's sounding like a proper trainer.

This might be fun after all.

She then gives us a cool down session and too soon the class ends. For once I really do smell and need a shower and a change of clothes.

In the changing room it looks like a battlefield. I don't think some of these girls have ever done a serious session before and they're dead on their feet.

"She can't do this to us. I'm phoning Mummy right now to get her to complain," whines Abby.

"No you're not!" shouts Harry.

"That's what a lesson should be like! If you want to dance then that's what we need to be doing. If you don't want to dance then leave. Go somewhere else and forget all of this because you'll never make it. Mummy and Daddy won't be with you on that stage. It'll just be you and your talent and if you haven't got what it takes then you won't even get past the curtains. Miss G's the best thing I've seen here and we need her!"

I think that's the most I've ever heard him talk and he's gone all red. I think he means it.

Peter Marney

No

"You can't!"

"Why not?"

"Because!"

"Because what?"

"Because everything!"

In case you're wondering, we're having an argument because Keira's being so unfair.

Miss G wants us to be in the end of term show that the school's putting on for the parents and Keira won't let us.

"Which bit about running away and hiding have you forgotten? Why not just walk around the town in a sparkly jumpsuit with a big arrow saying 'Here I am!'"

I hate it when grown ups are right.

Quite like the idea of a sparkly jump suit though. Gold or silver maybe. Jay the superhero, flying to the rescue of sick puppies trapped down a well.

Ok, forget that last bit. That's just something Red's been laughing at. She says Sick Puppy Syndrome's a disease some girls get from reading rubbish books where the heroine rescues sick and lonely animals but only if they're the cuddly sort.

Maybe I could rescue spiders and snakes and pigs and…

Naz interrupts my new career.

"But we really want to be in the school show. You told us to fit in and we're fitting in. It's what we're supposed to do. All the class are doing it."

It's taken weeks but we're finally getting accepted. The blondies have started to talk to me and Red, and Naz has other people to hang out with apart from the stick creatures from Planet Thin. We've stopped being the outsiders and started to be just normal pupils. Well, normal for this school which means that we're expected to perform.

"All it needs is one parent with a video camera or smartphone and you'll be all over the social media sites by the weekend as background to little Fiona or whoever. It's not like you're invisible is it?"

Well, I suppose Red's hair does show up a bit.

We wanted "Yes" but I guess we've got "No". After all, Keira's got to sign the parents form and I think the school might notice a forgery this time. Why does she have to have such an awkward signature?

Why is it always Yes or No?

Why is it always… hold on a moment!

"Naz, what's it your Mums say? It's never just either or?"

She nods and I've got half an idea.

There's got to be some middle ground. Somewhere or something that allows us on stage without the risk of being seen by the wrong people. It's never just yes or no and all we've got to do now is find the maybe.

Shame none of us have got a clue where to look for this phantom solution.

It's not even as if we're in the whole show. It's only the big number at the end and we're only in the background but Keira's got a point. One flash and an upload and it could all end in disaster. We mustn't forget that we've still got enemies.

I suppose Keira's going to have to make up some story to explain why we can't take part. It's either that or run away again and none of us want to do that, especially Keira.

I think she's got used to having her brother around and he's taken to joining us for our fighting sessions each week. He knows all sorts of different styles which he says he picked up travelling. There's this special kick boxing which he got from France and another style from Thailand.

Our favourite is a sort of fighting dance from Brazil which he's started to teach us. It's all spinning and cartwheels and done to music. Every weekend he goes to the city for special lessons and he always comes back with new moves or a new track to play us. Maybe we can go hide in Brazil if we have to run away again.

Keira's been thinking as well.

"Looks like we're stuck either way. If you dance then we risk being seen but if I refuse then people are going to wonder why. Even if we say that Princess here mustn't be photographed, some bratty dancer is going to upload a snap just to get at you if you have an argument with them."

Ah, that's where the princess rumour came from.

So basically, we've got to say we'll do it but end up not doing it and find a way to get out of doing it without people asking questions. And there was me thinking our life was difficult enough already!

I suppose we could get ourselves banned from dance but it's become one of our favourite lessons since Miss G has taken over. Seems I dance better too now we're all in trainers rather than those silly slipper things.

Besides, I'm not sure just how bad we'd have to be to get out of class. If we get too bad then it could see us chucked out of the school and we definitely don't want that.

Keira has got a point though. I know I can get lost in a crowd but I must admit that, unless they're trying to hide, the girls do stick out a bit and it's not just Red's hair.

Naz sort of stands out from the rest as well. She looks kind of foreign and in the right clothes could easily pass for an Arab princess or something if she doesn't open her mouth. Mind you, if she can act as Natalia then I suppose she could act as Princess Nazarina or whatever.

Maybe she could wear one of those long black dress things and a mask or veil. Even I could hide under

one of those and you wouldn't know
I wasn't our princess.

Keira thinks that's a daft idea
and for once the girls agree with
her. I'm outnumbered three to one.

This is where I need Wally to
stick up for me. He's the friend
we've had to leave behind and he's
really good at making plans. Slow
but good.

What would Wally do?

He'd go away and have a long think
about it all. He might be slow but
Wally always came up with a good
plan. Maybe we all just need to go
away and have a think.

Have you ever had one of those
problems which just seemed
impossible? Then you finally stop
worrying long enough to get to
sleep and the next morning you wake
up and the answer just pops into
your head. Weird isn't it.

Didn't work this time though.

We're back in the dance studio and still stuck rehearsing something we're probably not going to be doing unless...

Peter Marney

My new job

It's not an idea.

It's just a feeling and it's very scared so I've got to carry on with what I'm doing and ignore it until it feels safe enough to talk to me properly.

Just carry on dancing and…

"Ow! Look where you're going Jay!"

I freeze but it's gone.

Miss looks concerned.

"Jay, are you all right? Do you need to go and sit down?"

I nod and wander over to the side, trying to not think about anything in case the ghost of the idea peeks out again.

Nothing's happening, so I try to backtrack and work out what I was thinking about when it almost popped into my head.

It's like when you lose something.

All you've got to do is remember back to when you had it and then work forward again.

So, I got ready and went through our warm ups and then was working on that tricky step Miss has shown us and…

And nothing.

It's no good. It's been scared off.

But it's still out there. Somewhere there's a solution to

this problem and it's trying to find me.

Harry's looking at me a bit funny like.

"What?" I ask.

"I said, are you all right Jay? You sort of wandered off there for a moment."

Oops.

Now I can see why Wally seems a bit of a space cadet. He's just thinking too hard.

I make an excuse that I didn't sleep too well last night, which is sort of true, and get up to rejoin the lesson.

Now I've got Pink Hippo Syndrome.

Try not to think of a pink hippo and what's the first thing you do? Yes, there it is, wallowing in the mud. One very large pink hippo.

I'm trying not to think about our problem and, of course, now can't think of anything else.

This time it's Red who nudges me.

"Jamie, stop it!" she whispers. "You're going all weird again."

At least Red notices me looking vacant. Most of the teachers don't seem to bother and let me just sit there, provided I'm still and quiet. As long as the homework is done then they don't seem to worry too much about what happens in class.

There, we just sit and get talked at and let the blondies answer the questions. We also have lots of silent reading which is a bit boring for me as I'm rubbish at reading anyway. I just look at the page and drift off into a daydream until the teacher tells us to put our books away.

Homework gets done around the kitchen table and Keira does my writing for me with the girls giving her the answers. I help out where I can and they explain the stuff to me so that I don't feel too left out. Most of it's rubbish anyway just like the teachers.

I miss my old teacher, Miss S.

She was really good and I wouldn't have been able to hide at the back of the class like now. Between you and me, I don't think this is a very good school.

Keira's brother Jack is still teaching us this Brazilian stuff which is called something like "Cap-a-where-a". The girls are getting quite good at it but there's too much twirling about for me. I can manage a cartwheel or two but I just fall over if it gets beyond that. I prefer boxing.

Jack's heard a couple of whispers.

Someone's been phoning up the local boxing clubs looking for some kids who look a bit like us. None of the clubs know anything of course except this one and Jack made sure the caller was told they don't allow kids in the gym.

So, someone's still looking for us then.

Why?

They know who we are and know we've run away, so why are we still a threat to them? It's all very strange.

But if they're still searching then Keira's argument against performing is even stronger.

At least we've found a way out for me.

Miss G wants someone to run the lighting desk and Naz has told her I'll do it which is very nice except that I don't even understand the sentence.

I know I can run quite well and I know about keeping things in desks but where does the lighting bit come in?

Naz explains over dinner that night.

"It's simple Jamie. Mum used to do it for a job and I'd go and watch sometimes. It's really easy."

That's good then. I can do easy.

"They're all going to dance on stage in the Hall and we'll need lights so people can see them."

Yeah, that makes sense so far.

Keira switches on the TV and starts off one of the dance DVDs that Naz has borrowed from school.

"Ignore the dancing Jamie, look at the way the lights keep changing. That's your job. You sit in front of a box with switches and sliders and move the lights on and off."

I can flick a light switch. That's easy, but how am I going to know which ones to shift?

Naz tells me that it's all worked out beforehand and then someone tells me over headphones when to do the various changes. She also promises to show me exactly what to do just as soon as we're allowed to get the lighting desk out of storage. Seems they haven't done a show for some time.

When we find the desk, up in an attic, it's all dusty and looks like the controls for a spaceship with lots of things to move and twist.

Someone called a "Tekky" comes to school and sets up the lights and joins the wiring to the desk. It looks complicated and I leave it to Naz to chat to the guy while I just watch. Seems they speak the same language when it comes to lighting.

Miss G joins us and tells Mr Tekky what colours she wants and what effects. I sort of know what she's on about thanks to Naz and ask her to keep it simple and not have too many cues.

A cue is when you change the lights from one thing to another. See, I know this!

Miss then fires off some technical stuff at me and I nod, hoping that

Naz is listening and can explain it all to me later. Red can see that I'm only pretending to understand and asks some questions to get Miss G to explain. That's clever 'cos it looks like it's Red who doesn't understand rather than me.

Anyway, we get away with it and between us manage to work everything out.

Now all we've got to do is practise which is sort of why we're climbing through this window again.

Peter Marney

Playtime

Keira's decided that we're getting rusty.

I checked between my toes and everything but I can't see that I'm turning dark red and flaky but that isn't what she means.

We've not been using any proper ninja skills for a while and she thinks we need to practise.

The excuse is to play with the lighting desk but she also wants us to have a good look around the school as well.

Although it's only a small place, there're some rooms which we've never been in and so we're all keen to be nosey and have a poke around. Keira's told us not to break into Miss Rainey's files or computer which is a shame because I bet she's got her password written down in one of her desk drawers.

Naz lets me play with the lighting desk while she tells me what to do.

"We'll start with pre-set. That's the lighting we want when we come on stage."

She shows me the sliders to move and where to set them.

"Cue 1 means to dim these two lamps."

Lights are lamps in Tekky speak apparently and dim doesn't mean me, it means to turn the lights, sorry lamps, down a bit.

"Just move the sliders nice and slowly."

I do as I'm told but nothing happens as we've not switched the desk on. Do you really think we want to flood the place with lights when we're on a ninja exercise?

"Now bring in the side lights. That's Cue 2."

I remember this bit. Those side lights look really spooky.

We go through the rest of the cues and it's all done.

Time to play!

Keira's had a quick look around while we've been working and she now takes over from Red, who's been watching out for any unexpected visitors, so all three of us can go exploring together.

We're to treat the school as enemy territory, so we put our hoods up and move in single file, staying well spaced out. We know we can get out the same way as we came in but need a back up plan as well just in case someone else tries the same window.

We could pick the locks on the doors but it's much easier just to find some more Toy Town windows. A couple of the classrooms are near bushes so we make sure we've an emergency exit route. Always best to be safe.

We're upstairs when we hear Keira's warning whistle.

Something's up.

She jogs silently up the stairs to join us, explaining that a car has pulled up outside and two people with torches have got out. Keira managed to relock our escape window but, if they come into the school, we're trapped upstairs with nowhere to hide.

Why have we got visitors?

Did we miss an alarm system or something?

I don't think so. If we had then
the police would be here by now
with flashing blue lights and maybe
a dog. Now there's something to
look forward to.

In the dark silence we hear the
sound of the front door being
opened and see the corridor lights
come on. They're inside and not
worried about being seen. If they
come up the stairs I reckon we're
in big trouble.

Keira signals us to move.

We need to find another exit and
quickly.

The trouble with it being a small
school is that there's only the one
staircase. We might try climbing
out of a window but it's a long way
down in the dark.

If we'd climbed up then we'd know
the handholds but to do it now
would be risking splattering
ourselves on the ground.

Red points upwards.

It's a good idea. There's the attic up there where we found the lighting desk and I know how to get in. Can't remember but there might even be a hatch onto the roof which could be useful in an emergency.

Ok, it's turning into an emergency. Someone has turned the upstairs lights on and is heading up the stairs.

I lead the way and we're scurrying up the corridor and around the corner to the end of the block. The attic door's locked but that shouldn't be a problem for Keira's spy skills!

It's taking longer than I would like but we manage to open it and get through before anyone appears around the corner.

Why is someone looking for us?

Up the stairs, the attic stretches across the top of the whole building and there's lots of shelves and things. Looks like nobody's ever thrown anything away.

We keep moving, trying to get as far away from the door as possible and looking for another way out just in case we're followed.

There is a hatch out onto the roof and I know what's coming next.

Good job it hasn't been raining. Roofs can get very slippery in the rain and it's a long drop to the ground. It's a stiff latch but Keira gives the handle a strong twist and our escape route is officially opened.

Red goes first as she's the lightest and our best climber. She disappears and we wait. No point in us all rushing out there if there's nowhere to go.

A head reappears.

"Good to go," Red whispers.

Keira nods and we're all out on the roof in a matter of seconds. We'll just hang about up here until the torch people get fed up and go home. It's a bit cold but we're safe for the moment and the stars are pretty to look at while we wait.

We see the attic light switch on and shuffle along the ledge and behind a chimney. Who are these people? If they follow us out here then we're caught.

Still, it will solve one problem.

Can't be in the show if we're in a prison cell can we?

I sneak a peek around the corner of the chimney and the attic light has gone off again. A couple of minutes later and we heard the noise of a car engine starting up and see the sweep of headlights leaving the school.

Now all we need to do is shuffle back to the window and go home.

Easy.

Stuck

I'm stuck on a roof.

Again!

Why does this keep happening to me?

At least there's no dogs involved this time.

You know how I said Keira had to wrench the handle to get that window open? Well, there's no handle on this side and guess what?

The latch must have clicked shut when I closed it and now we can't shift it.

It's stuck solid and so are we.

This is where Keira produces a secret coil of ninja rope from one of her pockets and we all slide down the side of the building to safety. I give her an expectant look but she's not doing anything. Guess her rope's in another pocket back at the flat.

We all huddle round to discuss our options. It doesn't take long.

We could break the window and force the latch open. But then the school would call in the police and we don't really want that. So instead, we decide to look for other routes down from this roof.

We split up and each search one side of the building.

My side has got a distinct lack of doors or windows but lots of roof and chimney. Didn't they send kids up chimneys in the Olden Days? I'm sure I learned that at some school somewhere.

If they could send someone up a chimney then maybe we could send someone down. Someone nice and small like Red maybe. Then she can break back in and release us.

I clamber up to take a closer look but decide that this must be the wrong sort of chimney. No way will Red fit through one of those chimney pots.

Also, I think I've just found another problem.

I'm stuck.

I know I was stuck before but this time I'm stuck on my own and at a much higher level.

It was easy going up the slope of the roof but coming down is a different matter. If I slip then it's a brief slide down, a tip over the edge, and a few seconds to admire the view before I come to a sudden and messy end.

Keira's not going to like this.

"Jamie, you idiot!" she whispers, "what you doing up there?"

Told you so.

I share the fact that I'm stuck but nobody leaps to my rescue. So much for secret ninja skills.

"Maybe he could sort of slide down and we could catch him," suggests Red.

"And maybe he could just drag us all over the edge," replies Keira.

I think that's a "No" then.

"What we need," says Naz, "is a ladder."

Why didn't I think of that!

If I had a spare hand I could check my pockets for one. Or maybe Red's got something folded up and tucked under her hat.

Naz explains, and it's not such a stupid idea after all.

"Keira, you lie down and brace your feet against this bit here. I'll climb over you, lie down and stick my feet on your shoulders like this, and then Red, you climb over both of us and do the same."

Now all I need to do is lie down as well and stretch my feet down the slope and onto Red's shoulders and then clamber down over all of them.

It's not quite as easy as it sounds but we're all soon back huddling by the stuck window.

Back to Plan A.

Keira takes off her jacket to spread over the window and deadens the sound as she stamps down to break it, making sure to clear all the glass from near the latch. She then wrenches it open and we all slide through and back into the safety of the building.

I'm all for running away as quickly as we can but Keira's got a better idea.

"An unexplained break-in will get the police too interested. We need to give them a simpler answer which they can file away and forget."

That makes sense.

"Jamie, go break into Miss Rainey's room and see if there's anything worth stealing. Make a mess please but do it quietly."

Maybe I'll have a quick look for that password while I'm there.

"If Red does the classrooms, I'll take the lockers," says Naz.

Keira double checks we're all still wearing our gloves and we get to work.

"Five minutes max!" she whispers urgently as we split up. "Then we're out of here."

We know that there's not much worth nicking but make it look like we're looking anyway by tipping stuff on the floor and generally making a mess.

Miss Rainey's desk is locked but that doesn't stop me and guess what I find? On the inside page of her diary is a list of words all crossed out except for the last one. Now what do you think they are then?

I re-lock the drawer and then try to force it open with the ruler on her desk, which of course breaks. Got to look like I tried and failed.

Naz has got a couple of bags from someone's locker but that's about it for our haul of treasure. I told you it's a rubbish place to rob.

We force a window open around the back of the building and make our escape, again making it look like some beginners have tried and made a mess of things. We also dump the bags in a bush so nothing really gets stolen. After all, we're not thieves are we?

As an unexpected bonus we get the next day off.

Miss Rainey phones Keira early the next morning to tell her that the school's been broken into and that no lessons will be taking place until the police have finished their investigations.

When we do eventually go back I'm fed up.

Someone's bashed in my locker and stolen my trainers!

The good news is that Dog Girl's ballet pumps have also gone missing which will allow us all to breath easier in future lessons if we ever get back to doing ballet again.

I don't mind when my trainers eventually turn up but Miss Drama Queen refuses to wear her recovered slippers and just packs them away to take home.

I suspect that Naz might have had something to do with that.

Very devious these princesses.

Peter Marney

Dress

I think I'm going to kill Miss G.

"Jay, look what I've found."

It looks like another lighting desk.

"Miss Rainey said we had one so I came into school last night with my boyfriend and we got this out of the attic."

You mean I nearly fell off of a roof so you could present me with a desk I don't need!

"It's a sound desk. Don't worry it's really easy to use."

I'm not worried about using it. I'm worried about stopping myself from wrapping it around her head. I nearly got killed up there!

I'm not the only one upset at the moment.

We're running out of options.

The show's being performed in a few days and Keira's still not found a way out for the girls. Miss G's accepting no excuses for not turning up.

"You're either here or you're dead and if you're not dead then you soon will be!"

I think she means it.

I've got to turn up even if I am dead. I'm sort of vital at the moment as, without the lights, the show is frankly a bit rubbish.

Harry does a good ballet solo and some of the other classes are ok but our musical number at the end is tragic. Everyone's trying hard enough but they're just not very good.

The dancing's ok and so's the singing but put the two together and it all falls apart. I suppose it's a bit like trying to pat your head and rub your belly at the same time.

Miss has decided to make it simpler and we're all back in the dance studio. They're dancing and I'm listening to some music in the corner as I'd only get in the way if I joined in. Jack's given me a new set of Brazilian tunes from his last visit into the city and I'm finding out if they're any good.

Miss G calls a break but the dancers just grab some water and then start practising steps in front of the mirrors on their own.

I get a nudge in the ribs.

Red's trying to talk to me so I slip off my headphones.

"Is it really as rubbish as I think it is?" she asks.

What can I do? Lie?

"'Fraid so Red," I admit. "Those who can dance can't sing and those who can sing can't dance. If we mixed Harry and Tip together, we'd have a star but…"

I don't say any more as Harry's wandered over to join us.

"This is so going to be a car crash," he says.

I'm confused. Where do cars come into it?

I open my mouth but Red's already explaining.

"He means we all know what's going to happen but can't do anything to stop it and it's going to be horrible."

Ah, thanks Red. She knows I have trouble with words if they don't mean what they say.

"It's not all bad though," he says, nodding towards the corner where Dog Girl is going through the steps with Em and Naz.

Now she's got her new shoes, people aren't avoiding Dog Girl so much and she's actually started to try to be nice. I think Naz has had a long talk with her.

Miss G comes back in and the session restarts and they sort of stutter through the routine. It doesn't get any better.

I think it's a change thing.

Everyone likes to know what they're doing and we've all got our little routines. With me it's having the right coloured socks on each day but with Red it's making sure she never wears a matching pair.

Keira's up, washed and dressed before breakfast but Naz prefers brekkie in her jammies and then gets washed and dressed. We all have different routines and if we have to change then it sort of upsets the whole day.

With the dance routine changing at the last minute, everyone's unsettled and just waiting for things to go wrong.

Three days become two become one and suddenly the performance is tomorrow and we're doing a full dress rehearsal.

This is where we pretend that it's the real thing but without the audience. We get to see the costumes the other classes are wearing and what they're performing.

I sort of take notice but I'm busy with the desk and making sure the lights do what Miss G wants for each scene. She's helpfully written it all down but I don't want to admit that I can't read it so I'm relying on my memory and concentrating.

Naz has been through all of the cues with me, over and over until I know exactly what to do and so far it's all working ok.

Miss stops the show in between the scenes so she can talk to the various groups but so far, everyone has managed to do their bit.

But now it's the turn of our class and we all know what's going to happen. I can already hear the sound of screeching tyres now Red's explained the car thing.

Actually, it doesn't go too badly until one of the blondies throws up on stage.

That's not the sort of thing you can dance around so everyone stops except for the poor girl who keeps trying to show all of us her breakfast.

Vomit doesn't bother me at a distance but I can see some of the others holding their mouths as they rush off stage.

Miss G shouts for full lighting and it looks like the show's over for a while. We get told to go to lunch but nobody seems hungry expect for me and Red. Even Harry looks a bit pale when I ask him to pass me the potato salad.

Miss Vomit has been sent home and one or two of the others don't look too good either.

I spend the afternoon at my lighting desk but my class are back in the studio working on their routine again.

Red tells me later that Miss G had a right go at them and worked them solidly for over an hour.

"Everyone's shattered and then Miss Rainey pops in as well which didn't help. She didn't smile once, just watched us, and then quietly left."

Oh dear. That doesn't sound good.

Back at the flat, I try and cheer the girls up by telling them about the bits of the show they missed.

"Jonny's class do this really boring ballet stuff and they're nearly as bad as us. They've got some cool masks though."

Naz is unimpressed.

"Jamie, they're only little. They're not supposed to know it all yet, they're just learning. All they need to do is twirl around a bit and look cute."

Yeah, that's pretty much what they did.

Maybe our class should try that tomorrow.

Peter Marney

P day

It's P-day!

The "P" stands for performance by the way but I can see why you might be confused. Everyone seems to want the loo every five minutes and nobody can stand still.

While the rest of the school are having a relaxing morning doing their normal lessons, we're back on stage and trying to rescue a performance from the shambles of yesterday.

Miss Vomit hasn't reappeared and one of the boys is missing as well. That leaves two gaps in the dance routine which Miss is now trying to fill.

"Em, can you move left a bit dear? No, the other left please."

See, I'm not the only one who muddles these things up!

"Now, Kate, if you can come to the front and Harry, move into the gap please."

This isn't good. Keira's very reluctantly agreed to let the girls perform so long as they're in the background.

"It's too suspicious if we back out now," she said.

Now, everyone is having to move into different places and Red is right at the front.

Keira's so not going to like this!

The scene looks ok from the lighting desk and Miss G seems

happy. Well, happier than she was ten minutes ago. If nobody moves we might get away with it. Trouble is, people will be expecting them to dance and sing and not just stand there like statues.

"Ok everyone, let's try it all the way through. Lights please Jay."

I get to work and Miss G joins me by the desk so she can see what the audience will be looking at tonight.

Well, it's sort of better than yesterday.

Nobody throws up.

I don't know if it's a dance teacher thing but Miss G's started sighing like Madame.

Everyone comes back on stage and I hear Miss take a deep breath before she stands up.

"Well done everyone."

I don't think she means it.

"If you get the chance, go through the steps before tonight."

She looks at her watch.

"School's closing in twenty minutes so go get changed. We expect you back here this evening at seven o'clock and don't be late. Now try and get some rest."

She turns to me.

"Thanks Jay, you're doing a good job."

I can tell she means it this time. I can also tell she looks worried.

She's not the only one.

"Keep still!"

"Ouch!"

Keira and Naz are trying to tame Red's hair into something which won't glare out from the stage. It involves a lot of hairspray and clips and a bit of pain by the sound of it.

We've also got a back up plan but it's going to get me in trouble.

Basically, I've got to muck up the lighting for the routine and push as much red light onto the stage as I can get away with. Hopefully the effect will stop people from recognising any of the dancers and will mess up any photos a bit as well.

Miss G isn't going to be happy with me but I'd rather she tell me off than we get spotted by the people we're still trying to hide from. That could get messy very fast.

Talking of messy, our classroom's turned into a disaster area. We're all having to use it as a dressing room and we're all getting in each other's way.

Everyone's a bit wound up for the show and this isn't helping. Arguments are breaking out over silly little things and someone's going to get hit in a minute.

"Stop!"

Harry's standing on a desk.

"Stop it! Now! Everyone!"

I think he's getting angry again.

"The dance will be what it'll be and there's nothing else we can do about it. So just calm down and try to help each other instead of bickering."

Dog Girl joins in.

"He's right. If we don't help each other then it's only going to get worse."

If she keeps on like this, I might have to start liking her.

It's about now that one of the blondies spews over Tippy's shoes. I don't think she can help it as she's being sick and crying at the same time. Someone else rushes out of the room holding their mouth and Red jumps up to open the window. I do the same thing and soon at least the smell isn't so bad.

Dog Girl helps Tippy while Naz gets a mop and bucket.

With showtime approaching, I have to leave and get to my lighting desk. Miss G is backstage and will be talking to me through headphones as the show progresses, giving me the lighting cues.

Miss Rainey comes on stage and talks to the parents. I don't bother listening as I'm going over the lighting cues in my head.

"Jamie, go to preset," whispers Miss G in my ear.

The show's about to begin.

This is where I get a bit busy. Miss G guides me through the various lighting changes as the show progresses but I also get to overhear some of her conversation with people backstage and something's going badly wrong.

"Well, get her a bucket then."

Ten minutes later, and I hear her asking for more buckets.

"Does she need a doctor?"

That doesn't sound good.

"Who else can't dance?"

That sounds even worse.

I get a nudge in the ribs. Red's pulled some clothes over her costume and has come to update me.

"It's horrible back there. People are throwing up all over the place. Miss says we're going to have to cancel our performance."

That won't please Miss Rainey.

We're not supposed to know but Naz overheard her telling off Miss G.

"You should have stuck with the ballet. If this all goes wrong, I'm afraid there will be consequences. Perhaps we need a proper ballet mistress rather than a dance teacher after all."

Looks like Miss G is getting the sack and we'll be stuck with boring ballet again.

No, I'm not going back to standing like a duck!

It's time for the Red Sock Ninjas to save the day. Nobody's going to like it but the show's got to have a final number and it's got to be us.

Peter Marney

A change of plan

Keira's not going to like it either but we've no choice.

I quickly whisper my idea to Red.

"Go get Naz and warn her. You and her are taking centre stage. Whoever's still standing can join in as well."

I've just got to hope that my trick with the lighting will ruin any photographs or videos.

Masks!

That idea which has been too scared to show itself for ages has suddenly popped into my head. Arab princesses wear masks so why can't we?

I grab Red just as she's leaving to go backstage and tell her to borrow the masks from Jonny's class. It might look a bit odd but at least Keira won't try to kill us afterwards.

The class before us is now on stage performing their dance and time is running out.

I reach into my bag and grab my music player, plugging it into the new sound desk. It's not much of an idea but it's all we've got left.

I can hear Miss G's voice over the headphones.

"Jamie, we're going to have to skip our final dance number. Half the class have still got their heads in buckets."

This is the bit where I get thrown out of school.

"No Miss. It's all rather last minute but I think we can still do something and save the show. Just trust me."

I don't wait for her reply and turn off all the lights as I hit the music.

In the darkness, the drums kick in and I slowly bring up the sidelights.

Red cartwheels in from one side of the stage as Naz does the same from the other. They meet in the middle and start the Brazilian fight routine which Jack has been teaching us.

The music is just drum beats with this weird twangy string sound repeating and the occasional shout. Mixed in with the low lighting and the girls slowly spinning about on stage it all looks really cool and kind of spooky at the same time.

With the masks, the girls looks like strange creatures tumbling and intertwining to the beat of the music which is slowly getting faster.

Suddenly Harry flies onto the stage with a spectacular leap and dances around the girls showing off his moves. He looks like a hero from one of those Kung-fu movies leaping in to the rescue.

It looks completely strange to see the two styles mixed together but it sort of works. All of those mornings trying to dance to Miss G's beatbox has helped and Harry is fitting in his moves like they were made for this dance.

The girls break from their tangled web and Naz ninja rolls towards Harry before breaking into one of those ballet things which they can both do. Red starts to chase them around the stage sort of copying their movements but like a clown.

The audience are laughing so she must be doing something right.

The beat of the music is beginning to speed up and the dancers respond. All three of them start spinning in their various styles. Red's on the floor and breakdancing while Naz is kicking and spinning at Harry who's twisting and leaping around both of them.

Slowly they're being joined on stage by the rest of the class.

Everyone who can manage to lift their head out of a bucket is free-styling onto stage and they're all moving to the beat. The girls stop spinning and join in the mass dance as the music races and the drums throb louder and louder.

I'm pulsing the lights in time with the music, changing colours and doing whatever comes into my head until the music abruptly ends and I go to a full blackout.

Silence.

Total silence.

Then the audience go wild. People are cheering and clapping and standing up.

Miss G has gone wild in my ears as well.

"Jamie, that was fantastic. What on earth was that? No, don't tell me now. Bring the lights up. Everyone line up!"

They all bow to the audience who are still on their feet and clapping.

Miss Rainey climbs up onto the stage as well and it takes her some time to quieten everyone down.

"Ladies and Gentlemen, boys and girls, that was fantastic!"

Everyone starts clapping and cheering again.

Miss G's also on stage and she's pointing at me.

All of the class do the same and give a great big cheer to say thank you.

I give them a quick flash of the lights in reply and in relief.

It worked!

Miss Rainey is talking again.

"It's been some years since we've performed to you all and I'd forgotten why we make ourselves go through all of this hard work. Tonight has reminded me why."

I think she enjoyed it.

"Learning to dance is hard work. Day after day of discipline and dedication and for what? It's all for nothing if you never have an audience and never have the chance to perform. Well, tonight they did have that chance and I've never seen them better."

Neither have I!

"I'm very sorry that Madame Langley-Brown was unable to join us tonight but she's recovering from an operation she's been putting off for far too long. It will be some time before she's well enough to join us again but on tonight's performance I know that dance in our school is in the safe hands of Miss Gibbs."

Please Miss, say nothing. Just smile and say nothing.

I know that our performance came out of nowhere and so do you but there's no need to tell everyone else.

"Ok Jay," she whispers.

Oops.

She's still got her headphones on and I must have said that aloud. She is smiling though so maybe I'm not in trouble.

It was a crazy last minute idea but I think it worked and at least Miss G will be keeping her job.

With the masks, it looks like the girls have kept our disguises as well so it looks like we'll all be staying for another term.

No, it can't be as easy as that.

Something's bound to make life complicated for the Red Sock Ninjas. Something always goes wonky.

Wonder what it'll be next time.

The End

Peter Marney

The next book in the series

The Red Socks become convinced that their false identities have been discovered. Will they need to run away or should they stay and fight?

Yet again the Clan must use their special skills to save the day and rescue their new friends from disaster.

Peter Marney

About the author

Peter Marney lives by the sea, is just as bad at drawing as Jamie, and falls over if his socks don't have the right day of the week written on them.

On a more serious note, Peter has worked supporting children with reading difficulties and understands some of their problems. He is passionate about the importance of both reading and storytelling to the growing mind.

Peter Marney

The Red Sock Ninja Clan Adventures

Birth of a Ninja

Jamie's about to start another new school and has been told to stay out of trouble. Like that's going to happen!

It's not as if he wants to fight but you've got to help out if a girl's being picked on, right? Even if it does turn out that she's the best fighter in the school and laughs at your odd socks.

Follow Jamie as he makes friends, sorts out a big problem at his school, and discovers that his weird new babysitter knows secret ninja skills.

Hide and Seek

Find out why Jamie hates dogs and why he's hiding in a school cupboard in the dark. Has it got something to do with Keira's new training games for the Red Sock Ninjas?

The Mystery Intruder

Someone is playing in school after dark and it's not just the Red Sock Ninjas. Maybe Harry knows who it is but he's not talking so Jamie will have to find another way to solve this mystery.

The Mighty Porcupine

What do you do when your enemy is too powerful to fight? Has somebody finally beaten the Red Sock Ninjas?

The Mystery Troublemakers

Someone wants to get Jamie's new youth club into trouble but why?

Maybe the Red Sock Ninjas can find the answer by climbing rooftops or will it just get them into more trouble?

Statty Sticks

Why is Jamie being attacked by a small girl who isn't Red and why does he get the feeling that someone is spying on him?

Has it got anything to do with why his school is in danger and how numbers can lie?

Enemies and Friends

Why has Jamie got a new uncle and why does everyone end up hiding in bushes?

Have the Red Sock Ninjas now found too big a porcupine and will it spell disaster for their future together?

Run Away Success

Where do you run to when everything goes wrong? That's the latest problem for the Red Sock Ninjas and this time Wally isn't around to mastermind the plan.

With the enemy closing in for capture, the friends must split up and disappear. Is this the end of the Clan or the beginning of a whole new experience for Jamie?

Rise and Shine

Why does going to the library get Jamie into a fight and what's that got to do with Keira's plan for getting rid of him?

Helping to put on a show with Miss G was difficult enough without guess who turning up. Yet again the Red Socks must use their skills to save the day and the show.

Rabbits and Spiders

Has Red set up Jamie on a date with Dog Girl? If so, why is he now running around in circles? Maybe it's got something to do with the fact that the enemy have at last found them again.

The Red Sock Ninjas must use all of their skills in this last adventure if they are to escape and live happily ever after.

Printed in Great Britain
by Amazon